JUST BELOW

NOTHING

Printed in the United States of America by Apocalypse Publishing

ISBN-978-0-578-04692-1

Preface

There's a point when the pain in your soul reaches its peak and the numbness carries you just below the reach of consciousness. Where jealousy, envy, hatred and sadness have no standing and the only thing left are false memories of happy moments that never came. In this dismal abyss, empty shelled victims filled with a somber yet quiet madness, live out their lives in complete anonymity.

This book tells the story not of this realm of despair but of the arduous, tragic journey that so many have taken to get there. Everyday those lost in this dark place walk amongst us, whether they be friends, mothers, sisters or brothers. Ashamed to share their hurt or anguish because of fear of ridicule, judgment or scrutiny; they exist in a world of lies and self delusion to hide the pain.

Inside these pages, you'll see and experience the road they've traveled and the courage it takes to walk a path knowing oblivion is the only destination.

Table Of Contents:

Chapter 1: Education Through Pain

Chapter 2: Remnants Of Something Better

Chapter 3: Easy Way Out

Chapter 4: Bottled Up Inside

Chapter 5: Their World Through My Eyes

Chapter 6: Trees Grown In Hell

This book is dedicated to all those who suffer in silence but reach for the light in the dark.

EDUCATION THROUGH PAIN

A Room Without Walls

Lying outside feeling the air, I compromise.

Looking into the mirror, I meet my own demise.

Feeling the wind on the back of my neck I can sense the hate.

Admitting my faults I pray it's not too late.

Looking for my name in a book that was written before my birth,

I hold on to what I know, as my last days on Earth.

Trapped yet free, I sleep in the sewers of what I called home,

so many voices in my head, yet being all too alone.

Tears, an action wasted on one who has already died.

So I think of the hurt and pain of the others, in which to them I lied.

Lying only in self-defense, I beg I be released.

I stand over a man begging but he has proven five days long deceased.

The smell of him although unholy, seems almost sweet.

The scent of sin has risen through the horrid heat.

I bang on the windows of those I can't touch but with no answer.

This night has become like a cancer.

Sense can't be made of this tale if you think only with your mind.

Think now with those other abilities to which you the reader seem so blind.

Open to speculation or your words that fly like homerun balls.

Closed only to those who can't get out of this room with no walls.

Nothing More Than Dust

It's been a long time.

I watched my life and had no reason to rewind.

There was nothing special I had to see again.

The straight line from youth tended to bend.

Failures through puberty lead to disgrace.

Scars from ignorance were marked upon my face.

Smiles were quickly wiped away by sorrow.

Most kids had personalities, I had to borrow.

I took what I had, to make what I am.

I ate like a wolf but was simply a lamb.

As the seasons changed, so did I.

My entire existence was becoming a lie.

Loneliness and anxiety filled me.

Thoughts of suicide almost killed me.

So many claimed to know me but had no clue.

My mind is six chambers held together by glue.

My only difference though, is that I know your name.

My life never had one so we're not the same.

When I return to dust, please don't watch.

The worlds a clean slate and I was only a blotch.

All I Need

I need the pain that I once held inside.

I need the hope that the wounds once satisfied.

I need that stable hell that once filled my life?

I need that constant self-hatred that once made itself my wife.

I need that doubt which at one time stopped me from walking into the daylight.

I need the fear that once kept me from sleeping at night.

I need the criticism that once followed my ever action.

I need those complaints that at one time caused an immediate reaction.

I need today to turn into yesterday.

I need yesterday to replace today.

I need those tears to once again touch this paper.

I need that insecurity and its beautiful flavor.

I need what once gave me joy during my darkest hour.

I need the innocence of a homemade flower.

I need the silence of December eighth.

I need more than just the thought of a better day to keep the faith.

I need what I couldn't get from trying.

I need what I would get if I were dying.

I need the poetry to stop so I can forget.

I need a new beginning to erase the pain and regret.

I need to relive a life I lived so badly,

I need to make another mistake to finally be happy.

Trade

If you give me your heart, I'll give you my soul.

If you give me your eyes, I'll give you my sight.

If you give me your trust, I'll give you my oath.

If you give me your hand, I'll give you my touch.

If you give me a chance, I'll not give you a reason for regret.

If you give me your love, I'll return it a hundred times over.

If you give me your mind, I'll give you my thoughts.

If you give me your affection, I'll give you my protection.

If you give me your time, I'll give you my all.

If you give me your strength, I'll give you my spirit.

If you give me your breath, I'll breathe in your life.

If you give me your flesh, I will stick to it and we will become one.

Taps

As I write this, my left knows not of my right.

Such a simple mistake made.

Sounding so much more painful from a child's mouth…

Carrying on in this way, I live about my life.

Living a double existence yet still remaining one.

Questionable only in my actions, consumed by distractions,

like a woman giving birth, hurt by so many contractions.

One side wanting full attention,

while the other begs of pleasures I can't mention.

Short and sweet but bitter to my lips.

Soaked in pity, I release my sadness in drips,

Self-conscious but never conceited.

Drained of my spirit, the warning of the devil the only thing heeded.

Confused with honesty,

I say my real name…

Slave!

Yesterday's Sin

I won't say I'm depressed.

I won't tell you that I'm blessed.

I won't speak of love that doesn't exist.

I won't describe how I slit my wrist.

I won't scream my pain.

I won't confess that I'm insane.

I won't crawl for your sympathy.

I won't complain of a tragedy.

I won't let my emotions control the page.

I won't give into my rage.

I won't drink poison and yell suicide!

I won't whisper to you the hurt inside.

I won't build myself up by lying.

I won't show weakness when I'm dying.

I won't be your problem any more.

I won't stick my key in your locked door.

I won't drown because I can swim.

I won't repeat yesterday's sin.

While You Were Playing With Your Shoe

I'm sitting here looking at you.

As I write, you play with your shoe.

I wonder if you care that I'm here.

I wonder if you can ever see my tear.

I'm not crying…just in a little pain.

It's nothing new; I had it for a while.

Yet still, my every action should be noticed.

I feel neglected…

How can we be in love if we're not connected?

Am I just jumping to conclusions?

Or am I seeing through the illusions?

You tell me.

Don't answer me with a question!

I'd say it louder if I thought it'd get your attention.

I'm not upset, just concerned.

I would hate to lose the time that I earned.

Time I share with you and you alone.

To me, there's no greater joy known.

I wanted happiness, so I found you.

Please think of me as you play with your shoe.

REMNANTS OF SOMETHING BETTER

Sixty-Five

There are sixty-five spaces per line.

That's sixty-five chances to make you mine.

It's sixty-five reasons to make you remember my name,

sixty-five ways to make you understand my pain.

If all I have is sixty-four words,

let it be known death fed my last letters to the birds.

For I couldn't let go of the 13th of February,

I begged for forgiveness but wasn't given sanctuary.

I tried to give back what was given.

If suicide can give redemption, why keep on living?

There'll come a time I can't just look away,

sixty-five was the limit but nothing is all I can say.

What Choice Is There?

What if time would give us another chance?

What if we never had that first dance?

I thought I might write this to explain why.

But in truth I'm questioning the reason for this explanation.

What do I owe you?

What can you give me in return?

Nothing I figure.

As the days go by, the gap gets bigger.

I'm not saying I don't care.

It's just…I have no time to share.

There isn't a minute made for us.

There's no real honesty or trust.

The simple answer is to let it all go.

Roll it into a ball and throw.

I could be wrong, give me something better.

You want commitment, I just wanna be together.

Is it so hard to believe that this is right?

Is it really necessary to scream and fight?

We have a problem only time can solve.

Look hard and see the work it will involve.

It's worth it but can it really be?

If you make a decision, please write me.

What If...

What if things were different?

What if I was happy instead of you?

What if I said all those hurtful things?

What if we never put on those awful rings?

What if I could take back the past ten years?

What if I had given into all my fears?

What if we never met?

What if I didn't look back with regret?

What if my life was perfect again?

What if you were never my friend?

What if I had a way out, would you take it?

What if I just let go, would I make it?

A Moment To Dream

There was a point when it all could've failed,

caught between love and affliction, my spirit derailed.

Known only as the "victim" my real name was lost to eternity.

Lied to by so many, the truth became so blurred to me.

Using my misery as a reference I found comfort in despair.

Teaching myself suspicion of all, I sensed the scent of betrayal everywhere.

Not quite dead but just barely alive inside,

I gave up on hope and pushed happiness to the side.

Moving about only in spite of my fate,

I looked beyond my emptiness and saw a light at my gate.

Something so beautiful and pure its shine rivaled the sun.

I knew I needed to come closer; I needed these two to be one…

As my hand reached out, her essence took hold.

I experienced pleasure so powerful, it created a fire in a heart that was once so cold.

To connect in complete symmetry is the best gift known or given,

without a word being spoken, it may have been the best poetry ever written.

When I looked into her eyes I saw perfection,

a piece of Ambrosia that could've only come from God's selection.

In a world you couldn't comprehend, torn by pain,

I've found my shelter, my passion, my truth and my name.

I never thought I could feel again in this place where suffering reigned supreme,

Gone now but still by my side, I realize she gave me more than love, she gave me a

moment to dream.

The Yin and the Yang

The street seemed quiet that night.

The tears of babies were nowhere in sight.

It looked as though it'd all be alright,

as though the two families wouldn't fight.

How mistaken was I?

There were too many signs I tried to deny.

The blood running down the concrete,

visions of children walking with no feet.

The smell of anger and frustration...

Years of silence asking for compensation.

These were the symptoms but I couldn't see.

It's sacrifice that holds the key.

One life will muffle the screams.

If one dies, we will get back our dreams.

It's a lot to ask but there's no other way.

Change is what was lost in that stack of hay.

Now the only way to find it is death.

The only crime committed was theft.

For these families stole tomorrow.

Two families, one baby and a legacy of sorrow.

Stop Taping

Why are you there?

Stop looking in my direction!

I can't see you that well.

It's not even!

It's not fair!

Bleed you bastard!

You coward!

Take it all in now, reap the benefits!

Write your story; at least I'll be in the credits!

Somewhere you'll never be.

For the writer never gets respect!

Something you know all too well.

That's why you hide behind the camera.

That's why you crave the attention of the small print.

You know all the functions on the T.V. but you'll never use the tint.

Roam around in the shadows while your mind tries to get high.

I'll still be living well while you'll just be getting by.

Circling the same corner, the same trash,

you wish the strength of a horse but have the weakness of an ass.

The dirt is what you know.

Hell is where you can go.

Leave me be!

Turn away!

Release your focus.

Come out and see your victim!

Acknowledge your cruelty!

I'm done with this session.

Come into the light so I can give you a new lesson!

THE
EASY WAY
OUT

My New Tie

Last week I bought the nicest tie.

It had the most beautiful design that let you know why.

The colors were so brightly lit,

I wasted no time trying it on in the mirror to admire its perfect fit.

I wore it every day and showed it to all I would meet.

Every second of every week, it glimmered in the street.

You should've seen the expressions on people's faces.

Its presence instilled me with happiness; it helped fill in those empty spaces.

Smiles and hugs from all around were my prize.

I could tell they were sincere, all truth, no lies.

One Friday night I ate a big meal and hung myself.

I tied it to some bars above a shelf.

Oh how nice my new tie looked just hanging there…

I died that night but to the tie, nothing could compare…

Joseph's Beginning

I'm not who you think I am.

My name is Joseph.

I was born a minute before Chendel.

He thinks we're the same but I'm much better.

I can tell you all his secrets.

All the things he chooses to hide.

Why do I come out now you ask?

Someone has to tell the truth to his lies.

You'd be amazed at what I know,

but you'd be afraid of the dark side he doesn't show.

His poems are what I created.

I'll no longer stand in the shadows while my art is degraded.

He pushes me to the side hoping I'll go away but soon we'll be one.

I laugh at him in the dead of night just for fun.

I've been left in the cold to rot,

but ever so slowly I will take him out with a rope and a knot.

I'll be the strongest then,

he'll never be able to say "no" to me again.

I'll end his life and replace it with mine.

This is my beginning but Chendel's last line.

The Lights

I hear the train coming.

It's almost time to stop the running.

It's dark down here, so all I can see are two little lights.

The conductor will soon have me in his sights.

I'm going to stand back to the side so he can't stop in time.

The brakes will screech but tonight I will make death mine.

It's finally come to this…

My days are over and so are my nights of bliss.

I thought it would last forever.

Dreams that took so long to connect with reality only took moments to sever.

My place is beneath those wheels.

I can feel the Grimm Reaper grabbing at my heels.

Dragging me down but I'm choosing how it all falls apart.

This is a mental decision; it's no affair of the heart.

At the end of my road I see emptiness I'd rather not face.

I can sense pain and anguish that I'd rather erase.

The lights are getting bigger and it's all about to end.

I've given no real reason because I wouldn't do that to a friend.

My horrors are for me alone to bear.

Be safe and take care…

Don't search for me, for it'll be in vain.

Excuse me now, I gotta catch a train.

What Covers My Fingertips?

I've put caution to the wind but is it over?

Things seem different when you're sober.

The lights aren't as bright as before.

I need another drink, it's time to pour.

Don't stop me!

I need this in my system.

It gives you power and wisdom.

If you want proof, just ask my friend.

He's dead now but was so wise up to the end.

You take me as a joke, that's okay.

Laughter is how I'll make you pay.

As I slam into you, I'll smile.

I'll even do it in style.

I'll come dressed for the occasion.

You'll hate my entrance but love my presentation.

You'll look so cute crushed in that car.

You should've left me at that bar.

Don't be mad, it hasn't happened yet.

You have two more days until I make the bet.

If you have my drink, why is my hand so wet?

A Father's Goodbye

If I kill you, will your spirit hate me?

I'm not ready for this…

Who is though?

Maybe I should've thought of that?

I put my hand on top of what I believe is your head.

I cry because in a few minutes you'll be dead.

A horrible thing to say but you know it already.

As my mind jumbles about, my body remains steady.

I'm trying to be strong but I lack the courage.

Why am I so weak now, when I felt so powerful then?

I never thought there'd be a consequence.

I never even had a feeling of nervousness.

Now I'm sitting in this chair waiting to take a life.

Please small one…know that I don't hold the knife.

How bold am I, blaming another.

For it's my money that's taking you away from your mother.

A paid assassin will make it quick,

while I vomit in the next room like I'm sick.

Sick from the anxiety and pressure of this selfish deed,

all brought about through a selfish need.

My words are that of a killer.

Your blood is upon hands that were just too small to hold you.

I wasn't man enough to let you be a part of this world.

I hear footsteps.

They're almost ready now.

The time has come to let the execution begin.

In this room, will be the presence of sin.

Your perfection will be my loss.

Ignorance will be my mark.

Your mother lies still on the table asleep.

She wanted to rest, for in this, no benefit does she reap.

I wish I could spare her the pain when she awakes.

I know the tears from inside would equal the Great Lakes.

She never wanted your death,

I told her "I couldn't handle it"; words that now I think about with every breath.

Although wrong, I feel it's the only way.

Maybe a pitiful excuse but it keeps the guilt at bay.

It's time for me to go.

There were just some things I wanted you to know.

Rest in peace my little angel.

Tomorrow will not come,

from this responsibility, I chose to run.

I leave now because I can't watch you die.

In this place of passing, there aren't enough words for a father to say "goodbye".

What They Said Wouldn't Happen

This is what will happen.

This is the way it'll be told.

These are my last words before I get old.

Time will forgive me or die trying.

Some things have to occur, there's no denying.

I'll look in the mirror and curse my name.

Then I'll cut myself and take the blame.

When the blood hits the carpet I'll cry.

If anyone asks me about it, I'll lie.

I'll clean my room and put it in order.

With any luck I'll find a quarter.

This way I can call my closest friend.

I'll laugh so he'll never know it's the end.

I'll say "I love you" then hang up.

While I'm alone, I'll drink from a dirty cup.

Just a bit of alcohol to lighten the mood.

I wouldn't stare though; I'll be in the nude.

I entered this world naked so it's ok.

I'll leave the same way I came in, what more can I say?

As the guillotine falls, I'll not see another day.

BOTTLED UP

INSIDE

Lost Property

Just beyond tomorrow, I see a contaminated today.

There I stand, naked pondering an answer I can't say.

I breathe a sigh of relief in knowing I can't tell the difference.

I stand tall and ignorant in all of its magnificence.

The world seeming to surround my very being,

I embrace the desperation that keeps me believing.

Closing my eyes I see my initials in bright lights over a dark valley.

One letter seems out of place or could it have just been written badly?

I can feel the hate of another man struggling with my same pain.

I reach out my hand but he moves away and screams out "you know not my name"!

He fades into obscurity with the basis of absolution as a blanket of security.

In fear, I attempt to escape this hell but I lack the maturity.

Left broken, lying on the floor,

I plead my case with blood in my mouth dripping, ready to pour.

Staggering to my feet I announce my willingness to be blind.

For it's my own weakness that gave birth to this incompetent design.

My fingertips burning, as if to erase my identity,

I screech loudly the name of my persecutor but without obscenity.

Why curse a punishment so self inflicted?

The key to my salvation is far from encrypted.

The way out from this nightmare is placed before me,

It's a doorway made of nails that tell a story.

Realizing that dark valley was my soul inverted,

I wipe my name from its walls and deface them with something perverted.

Talk is cheap, so a picture will speak in silence.

If you bring together the loneliness and depression, they can make quite an alliance.

You'll have just enough to face up to your tormentors and laugh.

One plus nothing can form a million if you practice the right math.

These words say what I feel but encourage you to do nothing but question.

I beg you have faith that the truth is in what I choose not to mention.

I'm not a poet or even a great man.

I'm that short life line that resides in the palm of your hand.

I exist in a moment that to which I can't explain.

I wake up every morning to the image of an assassin ready to take aim.

If this surface has given you reason to take heed,

please understand it's these same thoughts that make me bleed.

I'm sorry I took back what was rightfully mine,

I'd give it all up forever if hope would just give me a sign…

Open Immediately

If I die before this reaches the hands of someone who loves me, rip it apart.

Tear it up because my lips fell to disgrace before they fell upon your heart.

If you find my body, lie it on the side of the road,

if the vultures come, cover me in gold.

That way at least my death would've meant more than my life,

at least then, the vermin that prey upon my soul can finally swallow my same knife.

My existence has no worth but the meaning can't be denied.

I'm the reason happiness stopped coming around, I'm why you cried.

There's no miracle in these words or in the fact that you received this letter.

I had hoped it would reach another but its true destination was never.

I've seen the cycle of things rotate and nothing is of consequence.

If you leave Hell to enjoy a piece of Heaven you'll only return to emptiness.

Joy is merely the middle-man to sadness,

denial of this truth will only lead to madness.

Forget what you feel or what you're owed and embrace what you've been given.

Open your gift of contentment and strangle yourself with the ribbon.

There's nothing else beyond the rainbow, the grass is the same as it is here!

Don't wrap yourself in dreams and emotions just to drown in a tear.

Take stock in what you have and if it's not enough, burn it to the ground!

Don't attempt to start over, take from what someone else has found.

There's a point when reality comes for the time you've wasted.

Give the world a finger and take what's yours because once it's gone you can't replace it.

Dip into the pool of despair and give it no chance to encompass your mind.

Prove yourself worthy of your name and make the gears of acceptance grind.

So many have fought to understand the gift I bestow upon you today.

Take up arms against society, there is no other way!

Before you opened this note, you believed in right and wrong and forgiveness,

bring about the end of your suffering and salvation will be your only witness.

I can't force you into this line of action but I plead that you act,

fate already has a head start and will exploit the strength that you lack.

Celebrate the beginning of something better and the abortion of all confusion.

Annihilate those closest to you so jealousy and hate will have no intrusion.

Once these things are done you'll no longer be a victim.

You won't have to beg at someone else's door for wisdom.

You won't have the scent of fear surrounding your every intention.

You can release your thoughts and ideas without feeling inadequacy's retention.

No longer will their judgment guide your every step.

They'll try to fight back but only you know where the gun is kept.

You'll bring them to slaughter for the treatment you've received,

you'll be the wolf, no longer the lamb as you were once perceived.

No more hurt!

No more pain!

No more being left out in the pouring rain!

No more having to keep it all inside until the sorrow exploded from within.

No more telling yourself it was your fault because they just wouldn't let you win.

No more writing letters hoping someone would care when they weren't watching.

No more beating your hands against the wall until suicide was the only option…

Everything It Took To Avoid The Screams

I can't sleep anymore, my past won't stop knocking.

All I have is memories of killers and addicts that kept flocking.

The pictures are as clear as if they happened yesterday.

I see cops and dealers doing battle for territory that wasn't theirs anyway.

The smell of dead bodies floating through the projects,

the image of so many young children with no prospects.

The streets nothing more than a war-zone for the hopeless,

trains and buses, just transportation for the soulless.

The water is polluted with the blood of the innocent who never had a chance.

Food is so scarce; the roaches are in constant conflict with the ants.

Women suffering abdominal distention from non-condom protection,

the womb, nothing more than factories for soldiers with a death sentence selection.

Hatred is the new fatal disease plaguing every city and home.

Tears are no longer a symptom of the disease but a prologue to the end of god's loan.

Families in turmoil, siblings raising arms to one another,

sisters no longer a relation, just a prostitute for their brother.

Screams and sirens echoing through the night,

the only thing sacred is the morning light.

In this place, I had nothing and regretted everything.

My only escape was to remove the suffering.

There was no relief in sight, so eternal rest was my best way out.

I can never forget but this coffin is the only place I couldn't hear myself shout.

Room 206

It's day twenty-three but twenty-four is already on my mind.

My family and doctors say I'll be fine.

Their lies attempt to keep me optimistic but the mirror is just too honest.

It takes away all the hope that their smiles once promised.

I thought I would live forever,

that the ties that bind my hopes and dreams together, time couldn't sever .

There's a patient in the next room and I always hear him cry.

Sometimes I wonder why they just won't let him die.

He screams for the end like an infant to its mother,

I close the door at night so I don't have to hear him suffer.

That will be me one day, I just know it.

You only get one chance at life and boy did I blow it.

I'd give anything to be outside living life to the fullest.

Too bad I took life for granted and ended up with this illness.

At least they gave me a T.V. to watch, but it doesn't have a remote.

All I can do is lay here and add lines to a Will I already wrote.

I'll never leave this room breathing.

I know this because I spend most of my time bleeding.

I hate to complain but this is the story of my last days.

All I ask though, is that you remember room 206,

and its last patient whose life never got a chance to go different ways.

The Answer

This isn't a contest just a competition.

I repeat my mistakes in constant repetition.

This isn't meant to rhyme so I apologize.

I've witnessed a sunset, now I need a sunrise.

Outside your home I stand,

I peer inside holding out my hand.

You open the door and ask me a question.

As you talk, I watch your digestion.

I finally realize I'll never be great.

For my time of glory, I was too late.

I turn away and begin to walk down the street,

I sit in the grass, waiting for the dawn to bring the heat.

Do You Know?

Do you know what it's like to wake up and be angry that you did?

Do you know what it's like to want to die but you live?

Do you know what it's like to love someone who doesn't feel the same?

Do you know what it's like to have that kind of pain?

Do you know what it's like to look in the mirror and be disgusted by what you see?

Do you know what it's like to want to change but you can't; you can only be?

Do you know what it's like to curse yourself to sleep?

Do you know what it's like to be robbed of all you are, even your soul you can't keep?

Do you know what it's like to feel your own skin and hate what you feel?

Do you know what it's like to always want to miss a meal?

Do you know it's like to see and read but never understand?
Do you know what it's like to always need a hand?

Do you know what it's like to hate?

Do you know what it's like to want to kill, not to wait?

Do you know what it's like to cry on the inside?

Do you know what it's like to watch lost love pass by?

Do you know what it's like to go out into the world and feel like a stranger?

Do you know what it's like to feel that your life is in constant danger?

Do you know what it's like to hold your cure in your hand?

Do you know what it's like to throw it away in the garbage can?

Do you know what the next question will be?

Do you know what it's like to be me?

The Plan

I've spoken yet never been heard.

Silence now speaking louder than my voice.

I burn from the inside to reduce the pain.

Diving in myself I see what has become a graveyard.

Living with a pen name that leaves an unmarked grave…

I look from within to the outside, to the air above.

A cool breeze running across my face is the first sensation.

Next came the results of living in uncleanness.

Filthy, I moved through the streets without the help of my legs.

Moving past the checkered flag, I felt my journey was over.

As I pass the finish line I see the line was farther than I thought.

Hearing the pronouncement of judgment, I look back.

As the gavel was hurled down, the verdict was guilty.

I felt my heart burst.

Looking forward I kept on.

Without a heart and having a price on my head I continued.

Dying but feeling okay about it…

Walking in the same path, knowing that if I didn't stop, I would die…

Opportunity was the gasoline,

ignorance was the spark that led to the fire.

I have spoken yet never been heard.

<u>Frequency</u>

The deepest words aren't what we need.

It's the simple things that make us bleed.

Anyone can create a new sentence,

a true master creates his own acceptance.

Loyalty to the old ways tend to creep in,

I give respect but recognize them as sin.

My only ability is being graphic.

Always abstract though, never causing a panic.

Many verses are written to amaze,

others use them to put you in a daze.

I only want to say what's been hidden.

I want to expose the filling in what's given.

The newest technique is yesterday's trash.

I contain contaminants but I filter the ash.

In one moment, a poet can capture your mind.

However, your salvation is just another line.

A writer is just an extension of a tear.

The potential inside us all is what many poets don't make clear.

Poetry isn't a talent but an emotion.

We live in a desert but dream in an ocean.

What I Am

I can't let go of the voices because then I won't be able to hide,

although I wonder what I'm really getting away with by holding it all inside.

Too much is never enough and too little will cut me to the quick with the power of regret.

So caught up in tomorrow, I've let all hope of today slip.

Doesn't this seem so simple, so ordinary?

A poem that seems to rhyme like all the rest but tends to leave me wary...

Although seeming to be fully clothed, these words expose me as naked as the day I was born.

Every day I think of returning to the dirt from which I was torn.

Can I escape a fate that is foretold daily by my own actions?

Or am I only destined to live the highest limits of my own low satisfactions?

Is there a way for the darkness to finally get lighter?

Each day I pick up my torture stake and plunge it into my dreams until they expire.

Every morning I fight against multiple personalities and the lies that make up my existence.

Each day I lose the battle but only by my own insistence.

I keep my words simple because I'm a simple man.

I'm complex in nature but have only what nature intended as my future plan.

To grow, wither and die in the warmth of obscurity,

thought of as a genius but my memory is smudged by the reality of my lunacy.

It takes so much to feel this but absolutely nothing to write,

I love the thought of forever but I pray for the day I can give up the fight.

Zone of Elimination

This is where it'll all end,

funny how your worst enemy is a friend.

It's my own fault for getting too close.

I should've maintained a distance like most.

Beaten by something so pure…

I thought I'd win, I was so sure.

Now look at me, lying in a puddle of pity.

The ends of my fingers feel so gritty.

That's from digging in the ground like a dog.

I was lost like a small bird in the fog.

Flying so high but not knowing where,

if I cried on your shoulder, would you really care?

You told me before and I wouldn't listen.

Now the life I really wanted, I'm missing.

I figured it was all worth the struggle.

It was all for a touch or a simple snuggle.

Sounds pathetic but it was pure temptation.

Still, I exist in this zone of elimination.

THEIR WORLD THROUGH MY EYES

Why Me?

When I look into the mirror in the morning I look the same as those who laugh.

I'm not sure if I really am though.

I'm treated like an outcast.

Isolation is my position and silence proves to be my only friend.

I should've never spoken up.

I should've kept my mouth shut and it would've been okay.

Now the hate rises with each passing day.

I think god hates me too, so I don't even bother to pray.

They say I'm unholy and need to be purged.

My mom said I should leave school, something she strongly urged.

She doesn't look at me the same anymore.

When she speaks to me, she looks at the floor.

I stare out my window at night and put my ear to it when it rains.

That's when I forget about the rocks thrown and the ugly names.

I've been pushed, shoved and hit but only a few times.

As I watch them walk away I can see the worst isn't over, these are just the warning signs.

Am I really so different that I deserve this?

To be held down on the floor and riddled with piss.

Just because I can have a girl as a friend and the relationship never go past the bedroom door,

but be friends with a boy and want just a little bit more.

I don't want sympathy, just understanding.

These feelings were a surprise to me, they didn't come by planning!

High School should be a time of fun, not terror.

A place where if you spray "Fag" across someone's locker, it's deemed offensive not clever.

If I leave now, it will all follow.

Inside of me seems all too hollow.

Having no one else to speak to about what I feel,

I have no way to help the wounds heal.

Although I secretly know of others who feel the same as I do,

with what I've endured, I dare never say who.

When I bleed, I wonder if my blood is the same as others.

My father won't speak to me and I have no sisters or brothers.

I think about ending it all often,

I try to think about the good I could do in this world but the force of reality, it doesn't soften.

This is one of those kinds of stories without a happy ending.

Not until the stupidity and ignorance of the world, people stop defending.

I'm going to stop writing now; I can hear the rain blowing in the wind,

I've already taken the pills; this glass of water will help wash away the rest of my sins.

Echoes of A Masochist

Another day, another mark,

if they only knew how beautiful it is in the dark.

They yell and scream and call me stupid,

they don't realize, it's these things that make me do it.

They think I'm weird or crazy for cutting myself,

they just don't see I'm the same as everyone else.

I can't explain my world, so I can only show you my pain.

Each slice is like a story written alongside my veins.

It doesn't hurt though,

I wear long sleeve shirts so no one on the outside will know.

When I go to school everyone's happy and smiling.

Sometimes I sit in the bathroom stall quietly crying.

At home I look out my window for hours with an empty stare.

My parents don't really notice my sadness; as long as I'm not pregnant…they really don't care.

One day I let my guard down and told a girl I thought I could trust.

I'll never do that again, I can still hear the rumors and see the funny looks I got on the bus.

During gym class the teacher saw the cuts on my arm.

She thought telling the guidance counselor would help but it just did more harm.

Mom and dad were furious but they blamed each other.

I couldn't hide anymore I let them see my scars, there was no longer a reason to cover.

Things are worse now than they were before,

I cut myself even deeper now, just to watch the blood pour.

Everyone keeps asking me if I'm alright, they probably think I'm going to commit suicide.

They don't see that it's not death I want, just to feel good inside.

My shrink says I have to write in this journal everyday so I can "express what I feel".

Putting my emotions down on paper hasn't made the vision I have of myself any less real.

When I look down at my body, I see nothing worth holding on to.

I don't think any amount of therapy can make right, what I've gone through.

I think that's my limit; I've "expressed myself" enough for one day.

I don't think I'll write tomorrow, maybe I'll just cut deep enough to finally take the pain away.

Please Read This...

Caught in the middle but not the cause,

I smell the blood on my shirt and take a pause.

Silence fills the whole house but it makes a loud sound.

When I close my eyes, I can hear it all around.

As I rest on my knees I see mom to the left and dad to the right.

It's day outside but all I can picture is last night.

It all happened so fast, I can barely remember,

taking the gun from the cabinet, two quick shots and an empty chamber.

Hours have passed and I'm still in the same spot.

I think of suicide and my only question is "why not"?

I know I'll never leave here, so I'm writing what I'll never be able to say, down on paper.

With any luck in a few days we'll be found by my neighbor.

They wouldn't stop fighting; I was the last thing on their mind.

I'm thirteen, an orphan, alone and out of time.

Let Me Go

Don't give me an answer, give me a cure!

Give me the hope and strength to endure.

I don't need your pity or excuses.

This disease doesn't stand still, it reproduces.

I need what you can't give!

I need the power to live!

I know it's hard to understand because you're on the outside looking in,

but I'm looking out and I don't see a way to win.

How could this happen to someone like me?

I've done nothing wrong, there's no reason for me to have befallen this tragedy.

Look at my face and see only half the pain.

I bet you hurt inside too, well trust me it's not the same.

You sit by my bed and say it'll be okay.

But we both know I could go any day.

With the advances that man has made,

there isn't enough technology for me to be saved!

I've lived my own war; I've been in the trenches,

I'm an all-star player; I've never seen the benches.

So many others have had it but now it's my turn.

I'd rather just die or go to hell and burn.

But it's slow and killing me in its own time.

I want death, why is that a crime?

Why should I need your permission to let go?

You haven't lived these last few years, you don't know.

What can I achieve accept to be another statistic?

I have no special talents or memorable characteristic.

There's nothing left but to end my existence.

Why does everyone try to keep me alive, why do they have such persistence?

If you want to see me at peace, put me in the ground.

there's no reason to keep me alive for a cure that can't be found.

If I live my life to the fullest, it'll be just half of yours.

I lived my life poorly and resided with whores.

I'm guilty of weakness, I have no innocence.

My family has forgiven me but their love is no defense.

For me, I've seen tomorrow and yesterday looked better.

My body has shrunk, my bones are brittle and my weight is that of a feather.

No Doctor is going to change my fate.

There will be no rescue today, it's much too late.

My choice, my decision,

it's my new beginning, my light at the end of the tunnel has risen.

Just let me go......

Young Girl Lost

She awoke every morning with sores in forbidden places.

She knew complaints would bring cases, which would end with bodies in dark spaces.

Tears were just a waste a viable fluids,

unheard screams and terrifying dreams were how she got through it.

She went from childhood to adult,

teen years were skipped as a result.

Constant whaling against walls at night gave her monetary value in the street.

Her status brought financial rewards she would never reap.

Mental manipulation from youth forced her into a world she couldn't handle,

everything good within her, slowly melted away like a candle.

Bruises across her face and body destroyed a once beautiful surface.

At one time fearless, now the slightest movement of another makes her nervous,

Her innocence lost, like an imprisoned statue in a forgotten garden,

no one comes to visit and there's no chance of a pardon.

Many days of drinking liquid poison gave false relief to numb the pain.

Her nose became a doorway for happiness so she could maintain.

Three days later, she was found sprawled out on the ground slain.

Not even a memory, just a corpse, no identity and no name.

I watched her life play out in a symphony of lust and debauchery,

but from my guarded view I envied her tragedy and reveled in my own hypocrisy.

For even though my words are that of disgust, my actions were that of an accomplice.

A witness to every misdeed, yet I did nothing to stop this.

She was the potential we all wish the best for, that never got a chance to shine,

day and night her death weighs heavily on my mind.

As the tears from the sky soak the very sidewalk that became her final resting place,

I take pause in remembrance of memories of joy that at one time covered her face.

A true fallen angel; a daughter to us all,

So free yet locked away in this casket with nothing more than "Jane Doe" written on its

walls.

The Wrong Kind of Love

Trust me I didn't want it this way.

I know I have a gun to your head…

You have to understand though, I love you.

Why would you leave love?

It doesn't make sense, you must be sick…

I can cure you though.

In death, no one can separate us.

Don't shake or cry…please…

I…I…just wanna be with you.

I'm sorry I hit you just now.

You tried to run…I can't let you do that.

This is our time now.

I apologize for the tape over your mouth.

But if you scream, someone might stop us.

After I free your soul, it'll be my turn.

Then we'll be one and you won't be sick anymore.

This is the only way; we'll never be apart!

I've never used a gun before but I have to.

I'll make it quick honey, I won't miss.

Just close your eyes and remember…I love you!

A Story

It's so cold out here…

I've been out here for two years.

Some would say I'm strong...not really.

I watch people come and go.

They look at me with disgust.

I can't blame them though, I used to do the same thing.

It's so cold…

I took everything I had for granted until I lost it.

Now all I have is this pen and pad.

Daytime is bad because I feel like the whole world can see me.

Nights are even worse.

When you're a young girl out here…

The guys I've met in street treat me like dirt.

But you do what you have to do, to get some food in your mouth.

even if you have to put something else in there first.

I've been raped but so many times I've lost count.

Guess you'd have to wonder who would even care.

I miss home…

I miss Mom and Dad; I tried to go back,

but who wants a daughter who ran away and came back filthy and violated.

I'm looking for a good restaurant right now…

They always throw away the best food.

It's amazing what some people won't eat.

I've been to so many shelters but they don't help.

A lot of times the workers there...the guys anyway...well...you know.

No one gives anything out of the kindness of their heart anymore.

The foods free but sometimes I can get some money if I do a few favors.

I hate it and I wash myself over and over again after but I always feel it's still with me.

I feel so dirty down there.

Trying to get a nice job…

Sometimes when I get a little money, I buy a cheap outfit.

Then I go where they're hiring.

But every job turns out the same.

I start for a little while and then some manager starts hitting on me.

I've worked in every fast food joint you can think of.

Every time it's the same.

He'll help me out if I help him out.

At first I would do it because I needed the money.

But when I stood up for myself, they'd fire me.

When I complained, no one would listen.

When your address is some alley or park bench, your cries are unimportant.

The rest of the time I'll just do it and just go cry in a corner later.

After that, I always quit.

I bleed so often down there…

I'm only fifteen.

But that's my life.

One day I'll be off the streets and in a nice big house.

A dream that I keep with me always…

The rain is falling; I guess I should find a doorway or good strong box for the night.

Some newspaper for blankets to cover and hide me will do fine.

I'm used to it; I just miss home.

It's so cold out here…

A Cliff...

As I stand on this cliff, I read from her diary.

If it wasn't her death, it was her words that inspired me.

Lightning struck twice but I stood tall.

As the storm rushed over my head, I wouldn't fall.

The sky was dark but the water was clear.

From the sounds of the ocean, I could tell a ship was near.

One of those big ones that looks miles long,

to me though, just witnesses to my terrible wrong.

A cup in my hand that once quenched her thirst,

how did I go from seeing her smiling, to seeing her in a hearse?

As she was put in the ground, I could hear her speak.

She spoke of the righteous and the weak.

Now gone, I commit myself to the water.

One death is an accident but two will be slaughter.

Once a poem, now a reality,

only time will do justice to this fatality.

TREES GROW
IN HELL

Street Incarceration

Forty-one shell casings still cover the ground of a grave no longer treated as such,

voices once united against the struggle, now gutted like the contents of a Dutch.

Streets of gold reduced to bronze,

six by nine cages filled with scratch marks of lost slave songs.

False theories of self worth keep the crabs from reaching the top of the barrel.

Isolation from the outside has made the way out, that much more narrow.

Talk is cheap but accounts for more than actions taken,

given every chance to succeed but hope keeps breaking.

Small bursts of light shine through the dark clouds emanating from fears and insecurities,

truth of a harsh reality put on the world's stage but filled with selfish impurities.

A sense of entitlement from a history unable to be claimed,

cultural differences distorted by ignorance and despair but no one to be blamed.

Tortured souls console one another while the flames consume their surroundings.

Adolescents scream in agony for something better, while their death toll keeps counting.

Mental starvation has brought about a change from academics to murder & A.I.D.S. epidemics.

Unprotected displays of affection have lead to the growth of infection and death clinics.

Earth's elements worn about the neck and wrists have given birth to envy and jealousy,

while greed for more has doomed whole families to destruction and tragedy.

A blind woman stands as judge with scales broken from the day of their creation,

caught in the middle of Heaven and Hell, many take solos in religions unconscious sedation.

With one fist in the air and the other in shackles, I pledge to fight what prevents my escape,

I've seen tomorrow through the bars, I just pray it's not too late.

Understanding the Problem

The sky is dark gray but seems almost clear.

If you listen closely, it'll sing to your ear.

Its song is about what's happening on the ground.

It's about constant screaming that doesn't make a sound.

The first verse tells you how we lost another son.

How he chose to fight, instead of to run.

You might call him stupid but "Nigger" wasn't his name.

The boys in blue thought we were all the same.

Come to find out, there's a warrior among us.

He was small in size but his voice was thunderous.

While others ran, he turned and yelled "no"!

He stood his ground; he had no reason to go.

With the rage of ignorance and judgment of racism he was beaten.

From head to toe, his bruises were even.

Who would've thought our protection would be our end?

If your ally is your enemy, whom can you really call your friend?

Self-division is how we keep ourselves from reaching the top.

The chorus of this song repeats these words and will never stop.

As the sky begins to darken, you can see the lights with eyes from above.

You wonder from so high, how can they really show love?

A dog that only watches is worth only eternal sleep.

Funny how death is in constant view but then we ask why we must weep.

The seasons on the calendar change but the year never does.

What could be, will always be what it was.

Might not make much sense but it will when you look out your window.

Try not to close your eyes as our numbers start to dwindle.

Race was never the point of this poem or song.

It's about how we shouldn't let our days be so short and our nights so long.

If your mind is closed, you might not understand what I'm saying.

To your inevitable end, you're just delaying.

For you probably thought I was speaking about minorities in the crops.

If so you've already lost sight of the threat and I'm not talking about the cops.

On the Battlefield

If you see my broken body, leave me where I lie.

Let the tears drown me so I can finally die.

The blood in my lungs only did half the job,

I'm at death's door, someone please turn the knob.

My sword lays beside me…my only friend.

The war is over but my pain won't accept the end.

I fought for what I believed but I failed.

I sought for absolution but that ship has sailed.

A massacre in the name of love is unacceptable.

My reign of justice has been truly regrettable.

There's no more hero's to march against the dark.

My skin has returned to the dust in the park.

My sins lay upon the bones of others.

Not just fallen soldiers but sisters and brothers.

I smell the hate that brought civilization to its knees.

In the deep dungeons of hell, the scent muffles the screams.

Genocide was needed to bring about order.

Tear soaked pleas from children were quieted by the slaughter.

I fought so long for peace but damnation is all I could offer.

Run

Someone's coming; all I can hear are their footsteps,

They're heavy like the lashes the slaves kept.

 As I run, I wander through fields I didn't create,

another planted but I took up residence as their bait.

I use the stars as my guide to freedom,

but the sky has turned its back on me like Adam to God in Eden.

My movements seem to stir more than just the fireflies in the grass.

I can feel my last meal from the pit of my stomach, through my throat attempting to pass.

My body gives in and evacuates its contents,

my mouth spews forth the lies of convicts born from convents.

Dare these words reach a civilized ear; they'd probably brand me a blasphemer.

 If it were up to me I'd speak nothing and take my place with the Grimm Reaper.

Unfortunately it's not death that's destined to be my eternal companion,

I'm forever trapped, isolated in a dark room that seems to just get smaller at random.

Never letting my guard down, I continue to escape my pursuer,

lost in a maze built for the guilty, I become like that of a rat and descend into a sewer.

Stepping through the filth, I soil my clothing in the very excrement I helped supply.

Shaking my head I deny my part in this destruction and turn a blind eye.

As I climb a ladder to return to the surface a small hand grabs me with strength I couldn't defy.

Looking down I see a young malnourished child with scars that would make Satan cry.

Thinking only of myself I forced his body beneath the water so he would suffocate and die.

I accept none of his grief and am too much of a coward to say "goodbye".

My head rises from the ground like a ground hog looking for his shadow.

I crawl through the bushes like the cancer through my bone marrow.

Knowing you're end is inevitable and believing it, are two different things,

that's what keeps me going, false hope can give a broken spirit wings.

Out of breath, exhausted and tired of running, I turn in defiance to face my enemy.

He's plagued my soul with incest, immorality and hurt, atonement is the only remedy.

He emerges from the darkness with eyes a flame!

As he comes into full view, I realize I know this man, I know his name.

He's been in my dreams; he's been in my nightmares standing over my body slain.

He has my appearance and facial features,

he commands my thoughts like mother nature does the smallest creatures.

His presence causes me to tremble but I won't falter.

It's time to give something back; it's time to make a sacrifice upon life's alter.

We stood in the moonlight knowing there would be no sunrise for either of us.

As we ran towards each other, we knew what had to be done, almost like a form of trust.

When it was done, I stood over his corpse as he decomposed into the earth.

His remains returned to which, to him gave birth.

I fell to my knees and wept into the hands that have just taken the essence of another.

The hurt ran deep like the betrayal of a lover.

For what we shared was nothing less than a dance and nothing more than violent fornication.

As tears rolled down my cheeks I began to stare down and smiled with great adulation.

I finally understood what he felt in his quest for my death.

He rejoiced in the thought of my demise and held no regrets up to his last breath.

Craving this feeling and turning away from all I've known, I start my search for the condemned. With my humanity lost and the thrill of the chase in my heart, the hunt begins again!

www.ingramcontent.com/pod-product-compliance
Lightning Source LLC
Chambersburg PA
CBHW050831180626
46814CB00004B/1565